#17 Dream Thief

#18 Search for the Dragon Ship

#19 The Coiled Viper

#20 In the Ice Caves of Krog

#21 Flight of the Genie

Special Edition #2: Wizard or Witch?

#22 The Isle of Mists

#23 The Fortress of the Treasure Queen

#24 The Race to Doobesh

#25 The Riddle of Zorfendorf Castle

Special Edition #3: Voyagers of the Silver Sand

#26 The Moon Dragon

#27 The Chariot of Queen Zara

#28 In the Shadow of Goll

Special Edition #4: Sorcerer

#29 Pirates of the Purple Dawn

#30 Escape from Jabar-Loo

#31 Queen of Shadowthorn

Special Edition #5: Moon Magic

#32 The Treasure of the Orkins

#33 Flight of the Blue Serpent

#34 In the City of Dreams

and coming soon

#35 The Lost Empire of Koomba

THE SECRETS OF DROON

TONY ABBOTT

Crown of Wizards

Illustrated by Royce Fitzgerald

Cover illustration by Tim Jessell

SCHOLASTIC INC.

New York Toronto London Auckland Sydney
Mexico City New Delhi Hong Kong Buenos Aires

For My Little Family, Wizards All!

For more information about the continuing saga of Droon,
please visit Tony Abbott's website at
www.tonyabbottbooks.com

If you purchased this book without a cover, you should be aware
that this book is stolen property. It was reported as "unsold and
destroyed" to the publisher, and neither the author nor the
publisher has received any payment for this "stripped book."

No part of this publication may be reproduced,
stored in a retrieval system, or transmitted in any form or by any means,
electronic, mechanical, photocopying, recording, or otherwise,
without written permission of the publisher.
For information regarding permission, write to Scholastic Inc.,
Attention: Permissions Department, 557 Broadway, New York, NY 10012.

ISBN-13: 978-0-545-09882-3
ISBN-10: 0-545-09882-3

Text copyright © 2009 by Tony Abbott.
Illustrations copyright © 2009 by Scholastic Inc.

All rights reserved. Published by Scholastic Inc.
SCHOLASTIC, LITTLE APPLE, and associated logos
are trademarks and/or registered trademarks of Scholastic Inc.

12 11 10 9 8 7 6 5 4 3 2 1   9 10 11 12 13 14/0

Printed in the U.S.A.
First printing, May 2009

Contents

1. What's in a Name?   1

2. What's in a Face?   21

3. Island Stronghold   32

4. Seeing Things   45

5. Tapestry of Evil   67

6. A Tale of Two Cities   81

7. Sunken Treasure   96

8. Taking Sides   106

9. The Battle of Lubalunda   118

10. The Impossible Riddle   128

11. The Jewels in the Crown   144

12. What's to Become of the Boy?   157

One

What's in a Name?

"Hush now," whispered the dragon. "We are trespassing on terribly evil ground. We shall learn a thing or two here."

The boy in purple robes followed the creature carefully among the tumbled stones, trying not to make a sound. But as a cold wind blew across the dark sand, he couldn't refrain from asking one question.

"Aren't we evil enough already?"

The winged beast halted between two massive, half-broken columns that loomed out of the darkness. "*I* am ever so evil," he rasped. "*You* are still learning. And so. We are here!"

The boy gazed at the giant stones scattered across the sand and wondered what had happened there.

"What did you say this place was?" he asked. "Messy Matzoh?"

The dragon shot him a look. "Meshka-mat!"

"Whatev," said the boy.

"Meshka-mat was one of the greatest cities of ancient Goll," said the dragon. "Sandstorms and war destroyed it centuries ago. These ruins are all that is left. Or . . . not quite all. Some of its powerful magic lies hidden here still. Now stand back until I call for you!"

The boy watched the dragon clear away

a thick layer of sand with a flap of his four massive wings. Underneath lay a maze of black and white tiles.

Muttering to himself, the dragon stepped carefully only on the white tiles, winding his way to the center of the maze. Once there, he crouched before a single green tile and touched it with his claw.

Suddenly, the sand shook, and a small pyramid of green stones rose from the maze's center. The dragon chanted several words, and the pyramid burst into flame.

Green flame.

The boy sighed. Magic. He had seen it before. For the last two days, he and the dragon had stopped here and there across the desert, doing pretty much the same thing.

Find the maze, say the words, look into the green flame.

The sky above was still dark, but he knew it would soon give way to morning. A very special morning, the dragon had promised. The boy would finally get to command a huge army of evil creatures. He would lead them to take over the whole world!

If they ever got where they were going.

Meshky-matsky wasn't even their final destination, just a boring stop on a boring journey of sand and stones and no fun and sand.

Plus sand.

Another cold wind blew across the stones. The boy shielded his face, then noticed his reflection in his armor and studied it.

He beheld a boy dressed completely in purple, with a shiny breastplate, long purple cloak, and high boots. He was medium tall, and he had stirring blue-gray eyes and brown hair that was slicked back over a high forehead. He liked what he saw, but there was a problem.

As hard as he tried, he found he could remember very little before a few hours ago. He knew he had fought someone, a boy as old as himself, but he couldn't remember the boy's name or what he looked like. And then there was some girl. But the one whose face stuck most in his mind was an old man with a white beard. Who was *he*?

"Prince Ungast?" said the dragon. "Come. Look deeply into this fire. See the ancient magic of Goll rise from the past!"

Right, the boy thought as he tiptoed through the maze toward the dragon. Ungast. That was his name. He knew that much. He was Prince Ungast. Dark wizard. Boy of awesome power. That was cool.

But it was pretty much all he knew.

"Prince Ungast!" said the dragon.

"I'm coming," said the boy.

The dragon called himself Gethwing. He was a moon dragon and very powerful.

Since yesterday, Gethwing had made a river freeze to halt a convoy of ships. He had conjured a storm just by moving his claws and had turned back an army by creating a wall of fire.

The dragon was also very old, having been — as he told the boy often — the most powerful dragon in the ancient empire of Goll.

Prince Ungast stood next to Gethwing, watching the fire burning in the stone pyramid. "I guess I'll have a cheeseburger, please. Medium."

The dark-scaled dragon's four wings bristled. "I am about to bestow the power

of the ages on you, I who was the most powerful dragon in the ancient empire of Goll, and you say . . . cheeseburger?"

What's behind that weird look? Ungast wondered. *It's as if he doesn't really like me. Or trust me. I wonder why.*

Gethwing had talked nonstop since they'd begun their journey. He'd given Ungast scrolls to read and memorize. He'd said they were going somewhere, a special place called . . . Banglebell . . . or something, where he, the boy, would be crowned "for real."

But Prince Ungast wasn't sure he trusted Gethwing.

Maybe it was the thorny spikes on his head.

Maybe it was his many long fangs.

Maybe it was the fiery red flash of his eyes when he was angry.

Maybe it was all of the above.

Gethwing made him nervous. He frightened him. He made him cautious.

"Look here!" said the dragon as the smoke began to assume shapes in the air. "I have asked the ancient forces a question . . . and now they answer."

Out of the smoke appeared large blue expanses that looked like seas. Tiny shapes — birds! — flapped across a miniature sky. Cities appeared on the ground below. Herds of minuscule animals zigzagged across the plains.

"A living map?" said Ungast.

"I have asked the magic how to find something I seek," said Gethwing. "It has told me first to go there. Right there. To that island!"

The boy looked at the island, but remembered something else.

Three trees. Where are they?

He bent closer and searched the map, looking for them. "Where are the trees?"

"Trees?" asked the dragon. "What trees?"

"Three trees in a bunch. Apple trees. On a hill. I don't see them."

"Never mind trees," said Gethwing. "You don't need trees."

"I like to climb," the boy said. "Don't I?"

The dragon squinted, as if he were pondering something. Finally, he said, "Have you ever heard of someone named Eric Hinkle?"

The prince shook his head. "No."

"Good," said Gethwing. "He is no one —"

"And yet," the boy said. "Hinkle. Hinkle. Maybe I *have* heard the name before. Of course, my memory is so very . . . short."

"True," said Gethwing, studying the map again. "Very true."

There was a reason the boy's memory was so short.

Ungast, young prince, dark wizard, possessor of magic few Droonians could dream of, was exactly two days old.

Not so far away, in the Upper World, three children — Julie Rubin, Neal Kroger, and Princess Keeah of Droon — sat at breakfast in their friend Eric Hinkle's house.

If Keeah had seen the boy among the ruined stones at that very moment, she would have said he *was* Eric Hinkle.

And she would have been right.

Ungast actually *was* Eric.

The boy in purple was Eric's evil opposite. He was Eric's dark twin, the evil side of him.

As Keeah waited for Mrs. Hinkle to finish making pancakes, she recalled the terrible day that Eric had become Ungast.

It began with a prophecy that said the wizard sons of Queen Zara would gather in a single place, and that one of them would fall.

Fall.

As in . . . die.

And so it happened that two of Zara's sons, Galen Longbeard and Lord Sparr, together battled Emperor Ko, leader of the dark beasts.

The eldest of the three brothers, however, the wizard Urik, had not appeared. Instead there was only a man known as the Prince of Stars.

But that hadn't mattered to Ko.

When his poisoned ice daggers flew at the three men, Eric leaped to protect Galen.

While he managed to save the old wizard, Eric was wounded. Infected by the dagger's ancient poison, Eric fell into a deep sleep.

Using the powerful Dream Crown of Samarindo, Gethwing returned from the dreaded Underworld and drew the dark side of Eric from his sickbed in Jaffa City.

After a fierce battle in the Samarindo streets, Eric's dark side, the increasingly powerful Prince Ungast, defeated Eric and took his place. That was two days ago.

Eric's parents didn't even know.

And the reason they didn't know was that Keeah was pretending to be Eric.

As she'd climbed up the magic staircase that led from Droon to Eric's basement, she'd murmured a changing spell, and by the time she had reached the kitchen, her long blond hair was short and brown. Her royal-blue tunic had reshaped itself into a T-shirt and jeans. And her pretty features had morphed into Eric's face, with a pair of glasses sitting atop his boy nose.

"Breakfast, Eric?" asked Mrs. Hinkle, sliding a plate of steaming pancakes onto the table in front of Keeah.

"Thanks . . . Mom," she said.

As green smoke drifted into the sky over the ruined city, Ungast wondered if there was something more he should know about this Eric Hinkle person.

He *had* heard the name before. He was sure of it. But when? And where? Eric Hinkle wasn't the face with the beard, but he *was* from before. Was Eric the boy he'd fought in that crazy dream city? It all seemed so foggy now.

Why did we fight? Did I win? Did he lose? Why doesn't Gethwing want me to remember him?

"Best to let it go," said the dragon, watching the boy's face. "You must keep your mind fresh for more important things."

"Fine," said the boy. "It gives me a headache anyway. But when do we get to Bumblebee? I'm so ready to lead my army."

"Barrowbork!" said the dragon. "It's my hideout in the Dark Lands. And it wouldn't be a hideout if it were easy to get to!"

"But I need an army," said the boy impatiently. "Right now I feel like a fish."

"A . . . *fish*?" said the dragon.

"You know, a fish out of water," said Ungast. "Like I don't fit in with the whole evil prince thing until I lead a big army —"

"And you shall lead your army. But first, I have a mission for you," Gethwing said. "A very important mission."

"Really? A mission?" Ungast liked the sound of that. "What do I do?"

The dragon thrust a claw into the flames, then pulled it out. It burned with a single green flame. "Touch this. It will not hurt you."

Ungast touched the burning claw.

His veins suddenly chilled. His heart raced. *What* is *that?* he wondered.

Gethwing answered his thought. "You feel the power of Goll in you now, do you not?"

"I do."

"Then I want you to find this." The dragon waved his claw over the fire again, and a shape appeared.

"It looks like a piece of junk," said the boy.

"I want you to find it, then steal it. You will make it new again in my secret hide-out of —"

"Butterball?"

"Barrowbork!" snarled Gethwing.

Ungast looked at the object, and his heart began to pound. Even though the thing he was to steal appeared very broken, he could sense magic in it. He wanted it.

He wanted, he realized, everything!

"You'll need a way to get to the island," said the dragon. "For your first real spell, why not create a way to get there . . . and back again?"

Ungast grinned. With the magic of Goll coursing through his veins, he felt huge, dark, and powerful. He felt as if he could do great things. Terrible things. He could rule the world if he wanted to.

And yet . . .

There was still the face with the white beard. Was the old guy *talking* to him? Who *was* he?

Ungast shook his head. "How about this?"

He opened his palms. From them poured a ribbon of black smoke. It blossomed in the air and formed a sleek purple balloon, with a purple basket hanging below it.

"My balloon can be invisible, too," said the boy. "For an easy escape."

"Perfect. You like purple, don't you, Prince Ungast?" asked Gethwing.

"I think it's my color," the boy said. "And I'd like some purple guys to help me. It's my first mission, after all."

Gethwing's eyes widened.

Ungast thought that made him look odd, but he knew it was supposed to show that the dragon was pleased.

"And here they are," the dragon said,

waving his claw over the smoke a third time. Suddenly, three figures appeared beyond the broken stone columns that surrounded them. They were rough-skinned, wiry creatures with long arms and slender fingers. They wore long cloaks and purple helmets that obscured their faces. Each was sitting on the back of a winged lizard known as a groggle.

"They look scary," Ungast said approvingly.

"These three warriors are from the Kindu tribe," Gethwing said. "Besides helping you, they are part of another mission. You don't need to know about it."

So, thought Ungast. *Gethwing is keeping secrets already? Doesn't he trust me? Why not? Could I go bad? Or . . . good?*

Time will tell. Until then, I'll play along.

"I'm ready to go," Ungast said.

"And when you return," said the moon dragon, "your true army will be waiting for you."

"Excellent! In Baggle —"

"Barrowbork!" said the dragon. "Today is a day that shall go down in Droon's history. But there is much to do first. Go. Put my dark plan into action!"

With that, Ungast climbed into the basket of the purple balloon, while the three dark warriors nudged their groggles.

In a flash, the quartet took to the air.

Keeping his eyes on them to the very last, Gethwing snuffed out the fire and soared to the east, leaving the ruined city as empty and lost as it had been before.

Two

What's in a Face?

At that very moment, Princess Keeah felt like a fish out of water, too.

Of course, she was anxious to return to Droon and help Eric. Julie and Neal were, too. Julie had even taken to bringing the magic soccer ball wherever she went, hoping for a message from Galen.

But just then, Keeah was most worried about being discovered by someone who knew Eric far better than anyone.

His mother.

"Eric, are you all right?" Mrs. Hinkle asked. "You look worried about —"

"I'm fine!" said Keeah excitedly. "No problem here. I love you, Mom. I love everyone! What a nice day! Hey, this breakfast is great!"

Take it down a notch, Julie said to Keeah, using the silent language Galen had taught them in Droon. **You're too excited**.

Eric's mother blinked. "Do you like the pancakes?"

Keeah cleared her throat. "Um . . . sure. They kind of remind me of gizzleberry cakes."

Mrs. Hinkle frowned. "Gizzle*what*?"

Neal nudged Keeah's foot under the table.

"I mean . . . some other kind of cakes," she said quickly. "I just love cake, don't you?"

All of a sudden, the soccer ball on the floor next to Julie bounded straight up into the air and floated over the table. Galen was calling the kids back to Droon!

"Yikes!" Mrs. Hinkle dropped her fork.

"Look at my cool trick!" shouted Neal. He stuck his finger under the ball and spun it quickly to obscure the words forming on its surface. "Pretty neat, huh, Mrs. H?"

"Neal!" said Eric's mother. "This is not the place. If you want to play soccer —"

"Right! Soccer!" said Julie, grabbing the ball. "To the basement!"

Mrs. Hinkle stood. "The basement? But Mr. Hinkle has just mowed the backyard."

"Basement soccer," said Neal, pulling Julie along with him. "It's the best kind!"

"Let's go, Eric," said Julie.

"Me, too!" said Keeah, jumping up.

Mrs. Hinkle frowned. "You three seem . . . different today."

"We feel different, Mrs. Hinkle," said Keeah. "I mean . . . Mom!"

As the basement door slammed behind them, Mrs. Hinkle called out, "Eric?"

The friends raced down the stairs together.

"Oh, man, oh, man!" said Julie, as they dove into the closet under the stairs and closed the door behind them.

"I'm so sorry, guys," said Keeah. In moments, she was herself again. "I really am."

Her heart pounded, and she felt tears coming. "For the last two days, I've thought of nothing but Eric. I won't believe he's just . . . gone. I messed up. It's all my fault."

"No, it's not," said Neal, tugging his genie turban from his pocket, unfolding it to its full enormous size, and setting it firmly on his head. Some time ago, Neal had been revealed as the First Genie of the Dove, but he was still learning the extent of his genie magic.

"We're all a little crazy," he said. "We miss Eric. But the sooner we answer Galen's call and get to Droon, the sooner we can help bring him back!"

All at once, they heard footsteps cross the basement floor and stop in front of the closet.

"Eric?" said Mrs. Hinkle, tapping on the door. "Are you inside the closet? I have to talk to you. Eric?"

Hurry! Keeah said silently. ***The light!***

Mrs. Hinkle tapped on the door again. "Eric?"

Julie tugged the cord, and the light went out. *Whoosh!* The floor vanished, and a set of rainbow-colored stairs appeared.

Without a sound, the children hurried down the stairs, away from the Upper World.

"That was way too close!" said Julie. "Mrs. H knows something is wrong! Good thing no time passes while we're in Droon. By the time we come back, we'll have an excuse. Hurry."

It was pitch-black, and the three friends could see little when they jumped off the bottom step and landed in something soft.

"Sand?" said Neal.

Keeah bent down and pressed her fingers into the ground under her feet. "It's damp. We're on a seacoast. I hear waves crashing on rocks. It must be an island."

As their eyes became more accustomed to the dark, the three friends made out a rocky coastline extending in both directions.

"Holy moly," whispered Neal. "We know this place. We're on Mikos, the island of Queen Bazra's fortress of stolen treasure!"

They all remembered the last time they'd seen the wicked queen who stole magical objects and hid them in her fortified castle. It was the day they'd first encountered Gethwing, the fierce moon dragon. It was not a happy meeting.

In minutes the sky began to brighten and the early morning fog to lift. They saw the tall black walls of the queen's palace jutting ominously up from the rocks.

The fortress walls were high, but even from a distance, the kids could make out at least twenty guards patrolling the rooftop. Each guard had two doglike heads, tall, alert ears, keen eyes, and long fangs. They carried nasty-looking spears with spinning blades at the tips. The kids had run into the guards twice before.

Those were also not happy meetings.

In addition to the guards, bright white searchlights scanned the coastline from snake-headed towers at each corner of the vast roof.

"I wonder why Galen wanted to meet us here," said Keeah. "And why he's not here yet —"

Suddenly, several shapes, tiny at first but increasing in size by the instant, soared into the sky high over the fortress.

"Look. Groggles," whispered Julie. "With some strange guys riding them. Ugly guys!"

Keeah narrowed her eyes. "The history of Goll is filled with odd beings. These look like Kindu tribesmen. Sparr will know. Look!"

Whoosh! They saw a flash of purple streaking past the groggles and dipping down toward the island.

"They're not alone," said Julie. "Take cover."

The three friends scrambled behind a boulder and watched a balloon, purple and sleek, descend quickly. Riding in its basket, his cloak fluttering like a giant wing, was none other than Prince Ungast.

"Whoa!" said Neal. "If it isn't the anti-Eric! He's got to be up to something."

The balloon swiftly faded from sight as it approached the fortress roof. A few moments later, they spotted the purple-cloaked boy leaping down from the roof.

"I'll bet this is why Galen wants us here," said Keeah. "To see what Ungast is up to."

Her heart was thumping heavily as she watched the boy who had been her friend for so long. Even dressed in strange armor and a purple cloak, even without his glasses, even with features that were stern and hard and hardly seemed to resemble her friend's face, Keeah knew that Eric was inside Prince Ungast, struggling to escape.

Searchlights scoured the rocks once more. When they'd passed, Ungast and the creatures scrambled across the rocks to the walls.

"I bet Eric — I mean Prince Ungast — is here to steal something," said Keeah. "Let's find out what!"

Three

Island Stronghold

Searchlights sliced through the darkness as Keeah, Julie, and Neal worked their way along the fortress wall. They paused at the corner and peeked around.

The prince and the trio of odd creatures were crouching together halfway between the corner and the main gate. Ungast was tracing shapes on the ground and speaking to the Kindu tribesmen.

"I wish we could hear them," said Julie.

"Turbans help genies hear all kinds of stuff," said Neal. "Here, let's have a listen!"

He stretched out his turban to fit over all three of their heads. Instantly, they could hear Ungast's words loud and clear.

"Did you bring the chains?" he asked.

One of the creatures nodded.

"Very good," said the dark prince. "Now, I know you Kindu guys are from Goll or whatever, but watch this. I picked up some awesome power back at Messy Mitts, and I want to try it out."

Flapping his cloak over his shoulders, Prince Ungast drew a large circle on the wall with his finger. As his finger traced the stone, it left a narrow line of green flame behind it. When the circle was complete, Ungast murmured a few words, smiled, puffed up his cheeks, and blew directly at the flaming circle.

The stones flared suddenly, and the flames flickered out, revealing a hole in the wall large enough to step through.

The dark beings nodded their heads.

"I know, right?" said Ungast. "Gethwing gave me a whole hunk of Goll power. I'm pretty much amazing now."

"Eric could not do that!" whispered Julie.

"No kidding," said Neal. "Ungast learned some strong new magic."

"Old magic," said Keeah with a frown. "Green flame comes from only one place: the dark empire of Goll. Gethwing must have bestowed this ability on him in the past two days. Ungast is more powerful than he was in Samarindo. Much more powerful."

Ungast jumped through the hole. The dark creatures followed him inside.

The three friends waited a minute or two, then Keeah stood. "Our turn."

"Nice of him to leave the door open," Neal commented.

Together the children crept cautiously along the base of the wall and hopped through the hole Ungast had made. They found themselves in a vast gallery filled with treasures from every province of Droon and from every era of its long history.

Inside the fortress, it was hushed except for the distant echo of heavy footsteps.

"Guards," whispered Julie, darting across the gallery. "Ungast went that way. Hurry."

To Keeah the rooms smelled like the domain of history itself. As they moved deeper into the fortress, she recognized long-lost treasures and precious artifacts among the stolen objects and wished she could return them to their owners.

Another time, she thought. *Not now*.

The kids hastened through the passages until they saw a glimmer of green light shining from a room to their left.

"Aha," whispered Neal. "Careful . . . "

Peeking in, the children spotted Prince Ungast staring at a golden door on the far side of the room. The Kindu tribesmen, meanwhile, were rummaging through a display of old weapons.

Ungast turned to watch them take three different objects — a wavy-bladed dagger, a wooden ball with spikes coming from it, and a pair of silver boots — and hide them in the sacks hanging over their shoulders.

"What are those dudes up to?" asked Neal.

"I'm sure those treasures come from ancient Goll," whispered Keeah. "Remember what they are."

With the flick of a finger and the stamp of a foot, Prince Ungast made the golden door open. He grinned back at the three tribesmen.

"Come on," he said. "Now it's time for *my* mission."

Together, they entered a room piled high with the litter of battle — dented helmets and twisted spears, cracked shields and broken staffs, fragments of swords and spears and armor, some gleaming as if new, some rusted.

The children watched Ungast stride up to an enormous statue of Lord Sparr as a younger man. A spiked helmet sat on the sorcerer's head. Fearsome jagged fins grew out from behind his ears. His trademark black cloak reached the ground. His iron fists were ready for battle. And his steely eyes focused on the faraway distance, as if he stared into the future itself.

"That thing scares me," whispered Neal.

"It scares all of us," said Julie. "That was Sparr when he was really evil. Shhh . . ."

Ungast shook his head and stepped through the artifacts until he came to a crumpled heap of yellow metal, twisted and burned and crushed.

It was a complete wreck.

But there was no mistaking what it was.

"Lord Sparr's old car!" whispered Keeah.

Neal and Julie remembered the first time they had ever seen the strange car, so very long ago.

It was in a deep, dark forest.

Lord Sparr had used it to chase Keeah across Droon and had finally trapped her in the forest. The kids' first mission in Droon was to rescue her from Sparr's forbidden city of Plud.

"Why does Ungast want that?" Julie whispered.

"Let's find out," said Keeah.

The kids crept into the room and hid behind the statue of Sparr.

"Attach the chain," Ungast said, looking straight up at the ceiling. "I'll be on the rooftop. We'll lift the car out through there."

Again, the warriors nodded silently. They went to work attaching one end of the chain to the car. Ungast pointed a finger and — *poomf!* — the other end of the chain rose up in the air as stiffly as a column of iron.

"Now be amazed!" Ungast clutched the chain, and it rose to the ceiling. When he reached the top, he drew a circle on the ceiling and whispered the same words as before. The circle vanished in a wisp of green fire like the first one. He climbed through the hole and onto the roof.

"Ungast is very powerful," whispered Keeah. "I doubt even I could do that. But why does he want Sparr's wreck?"

"Let's follow him. Come fly with us," Julie said to Keeah.

As the dark tribesmen continued to grapple with the car, Neal and Julie held Keeah's hands and silently flew her up to the ceiling, where they slipped outside.

The section of the rooftop they found themselves on was directly in the shadow of one of the search towers. Ungast was several feet away, attaching the chain to something invisible.

"He's using the balloon to steal the car," said Keeah, forgetting to keep her voice down.

Ungast whirled around on his heels. "Who's there?" he whispered.

Keeah's fingertips sparked. In the violet light, she saw Ungast's cold, hard features as his eyes met hers. She tried to imagine the face of her friend behind those features.

Ungast snarled. "I know you!"

Keeah's heart skipped a beat. "Really? You know me?"

The boy cracked a wicked smile. "Sure. You're the princess who discovers Queen Bazra's legendary black dungeon!"

"Legendary black dungeon?" Neal repeated. He looked puzzled. "Why would she discover that?"

Laughing, Ungast tossed a ball of

sizzling fire up into the air. In his hands —
whoomp! — appeared a narrow length
of wood.

"A baseball bat?" said Julie.

Ungast swung the bat at the fireball,
and it struck the search tower with a
loud crash.

The guards inside began to shout.
"Thieves! On the rooftop!"

"And that's how you discover the dungeon," said Ungast. "Gotta run!"

"Eric!" Keeah said suddenly. "Wait —"

Alarms wailed from inside the fortress.
The shouts of the dog-headed guards
echoed across the rooftop.

"Let's get out of here!" said Neal.

"Me first!" Ungast pulled on the chain,
and the nearly invisible outline of his purple balloon formed out of the air. He jumped
into its basket, and it rose quickly. As it did,
the crumpled hulk of Sparr's automobile

appeared through the hole in the roof. Before the kids had time to react, Ungast, the balloon, and the car were floating swiftly away.

"Halt! Thieves!" The two-headed guards raced down the tower after the kids. Their many-pointed spears whirled angrily.

"Hurry to the water!" said Keeah. "Oh, Galen, where are you?"

"Get them!" barked the guards.

"No, don't!" said Neal. He, Keeah, and Julie joined hands and jumped off the rooftop as a swarm of angry spears spun at them.

From his safe perch in his hot-air balloon, Ungast laughed.

Four

Seeing Things

Flang! Whong! Spears crashed against the rocks as the kids landed roughly at the foot of the walls. In no time, another troop of Bazra's dog-headed guards rushed from the main gate. The kids raced to the shore.

"Those guards move really fast!" said Neal.

"So move faster!" said Keeah. She shot a spray of violet sparks across the rocks, sending the guards scurrying and giving the kids time to get to the beach.

"But where's Galen?" asked Julie.

Keeah scanned the sea until she spotted a bright blue ship racing across the water toward them. "It's the *Jaffa Wind*! Galen's coming for us!"

She blasted at the guards once more and pulled her friends to the edge of the water.

"Galen, hurry!" cried Julie.

But when they saw a wizard standing on his head and turning the ship's wheel with his feet, they realized it wasn't Galen.

It was the wizard's opposite, Nelag.

The children loved and trusted Nelag, even though he had no real powers of his own and acted and spoke in opposites.

With great effort, Nelag slid the *Jaffa*

Wind right up onto the sand, and the children hopped aboard. The fortress guards growled and ran faster, throwing their spears at the ship, but a thunderous chug from its steam engine pushed the *Jaffa Wind* straight back out to sea and to safety.

"We expected Galen," said Julie.

Nelag patted the children's heads one by one and said, "I do not have a message from my opposite, that strange bearded fellow."

"Please tell us," said Keeah.

"No," said the pretend wizard, unrolling a little scroll and reading from it.

"Ahem. Galen Longbeard says, 'I cannot meet you, so I send a friend in my place. Things have changed since you were in the Upper World. Gethwing is gathering to his evil lair of Barrowbork the largest army of beasts seen since the fall of the Goll empire. He intends to wage a war we cannot win!'"

"Please continue," said Keeah.

"'King Zello has gone to defend the Oobja people against a wingwolf attack. Queen Relna's navy was frozen in the Kubar River. Sparr, Max, and I are riding to Zorfendorf Castle to consult the ancient texts. Nelag will bring you there through the Rivertangle valley. Our goal must be to bring Eric back to us. That is our only chance of victory against the dragon!'"

Nelag chuckled. "That makes no sense!"

To the children, it made perfect sense.

"Gethwing used Ko's prophecy for his own purposes," said Neal. "Even though the prophecy didn't come true, Gethwing saw his chance to turn Eric to the dark side."

"And now he's using Eric to help him win," said Julie.

Keeah hoped against hope that they could bring Eric back. But when she thought about her friend, she pictured him wandering lost and alone in the middle of the Dark Lands, and the way to him was long, winding, and dangerous.

And maybe impossible.

"The books and scrolls at Zorfendorf may tell us how to bring Eric back," said Keeah.

"We love Eric," said Julie. "We'll do what we need to do."

"Neither will I," said Nelag, pointing up. "Don't look there!"

Something bright and noisy was flashing across the sky exactly where he pointed. It was a flying carpet traveling at great speed.

And it was out of control.

"Heeeeelp!" cried a little voice. The carpet suddenly flipped over and dived at the ship.

"It's Max!" said Julie. "Watch out!"

At the last second, the spider troll jerked the carpet right side up. It thudded onto the deck and skidded into Nelag, pinning him against the mast.

"Well done!" said the pretend wizard.

"Max, are you all right?" asked Julie.

Max staggered to his feet and shook himself all over like a wet dog. "Cheap carpet!" he grumbled. "It's certainly not a Pasha original. But it's all I could find."

"What news, Max?" Keeah asked anxiously.

"My friends," Max said, shaking his head sadly, "beasts are gathering all across Droon. Plus, I had to use a second-rate flyer! But that's not the news. The news is that on our way to Zorfendorf, Galen, Sparr, and I were attacked! A rogue band of Ninns surprised us on the road. I barely managed to escape on this thing. You must come at once!"

"We'll go right now!" said Julie.

"Nelag," said Keeah. "Please take good care of yourself and of the ship. We may need you sooner than we think!"

The backward wizard saluted. "I promise to sink the boat the first chance I get."

The children knew this meant that he would guard the ship with his life.

The three friends jumped onto Max's carpet. Its fringes were frayed, and there was a rip across one side and a hole in the middle.

"I hope this holds us all," said Neal.

"I doubt it will," said Max. "But it's all we have. Hold one another tight. And . . . up we go!"

Clinging to the flying carpet's fringes, the little crew skidded across the ship's deck and lurched into the brightening morning sky.

It was a bumpy ride.

Max had often told the children he was not meant for heights. He was not a good pilot.

"Max, four of us began this flight," said Neal, clutching the carpet with both hands. "How about we finish with all four?"

"Interesting idea," said Max. He tugged the corner with all his might, and it came off in his hands. "Uh-oh. Everyone lean to the left!"

They did, and the carpet immediately fell twenty feet.

"I mean right!" cried Max.

They obeyed, and the carpet leveled out, but just barely. Julie, Neal, and Keeah clung to the torn fabric with all their strength.

Soon the western coast of Droon rolled beneath them. As Max turned south toward Zorfendorf, the travelers spotted flashes of blue sparks over the convergence of waters known as Rivertangle.

"Down there! It's Galen!" said Julie.

"He and Sparr must be escaping to the plains," said Keeah. "Max, hurry!"

"I'll try," he said. Gritting his teeth, he yanked the carpet suddenly, and it plunged down, skimming the rushing waters.

"There they are — " cried Neal.

A pair of pilkas tied to a small cart was galloping wildly along the winding river-bank. In the cart sat Sparr, shrouded and hunched over as if asleep, and Galen, snapping the reins and prodding the pilkas to go faster.

Hundreds of Ninns, some riding horned beasts, others charging on foot, pursued the two sons of Zara along the riverbank.

Galen fired back, sending short streams of pale blue sparks at the red-faced attackers. But the Ninns were steadily gaining on the cart.

"Bad Ninns!" cried Julie. "Gethwing must have lured them with his power."

"Max, can you distract them?" asked Keeah. "Lead them away from the cart when I blast."

"Aye aye!" Max wiggled its fringes, and the carpet swooped between the reeds, then arched up behind the Ninns as Keeah sprayed sizzling sparks.

Blam! Blam!

The Ninns whirled around and began firing flaming arrows at the carpet.

Neal and Julie leaned from side to side, dodging the arrows, as Keeah aimed her fingers and sent a stream of hot violet sparks at the Ninns, scattering them.

As the carpet zoomed overhead, Neal blew a cloud of bad-smelling fog onto the clumsy warriors, causing them to stop in their tracks, cough wildly, and, finally, to flee.

Galen slowed the cart till it stopped. "Thank you, friends! Our red-faced enemies have left for the moment, but Gethwing continues to draw every evil creature to his cause — oh, my brother!"

Sparr suddenly sank to the floor of the cart, gasping for breath.

"Brother, are you all right?" asked Galen, kneeling next to him.

Sparr nodded. "I am. And you?"

"For now," said the bearded wizard.

It was touching to see the two brothers, who had been enemies for so long, so concerned about each other. But Keeah sensed in their words a trace of something larger and more dangerous to come.

Sparr had aged since his time in the Underworld. He was old, blind, weak, and nearly powerless.

But his spirit, Keeah knew, was strong.

For now.

As Keeah gazed at the two brothers, she noticed that Galen was clutching a tiny swatch of fabric. It was orange, with silvery threads running through it.

When the old wizard saw Keeah looking at it, he hid it away in the depths of his cloak.

The spider troll cleared his throat. "If Zorfendorf is too far and the plains not safe from the old Goll magic, I think . . .

I think there is only one place to hide. Lubalunda!"

"Where's that?" asked Neal.

Galen shook his head. "The spider troll village? No, no. It has escaped war for so long. Let us find another place. We risk bringing violence into the home of peaceful people."

Max stepped up to his lifelong friend. "I know my people. They would invite us into their hilltop sanctuary if they knew we had no choice. My people will defend us no matter the cost. Trust me. Let's head for the hills!"

No matter the cost. The words startled Keeah. She dreaded thinking about what the cost would be.

"It's been many years, but I still know the way," said Max. "Shall we go?"

Galen looked at Sparr, then at the children. "And so we see the nobility and bravery of the spider troll people. Max, lead us into your secret mountain home. We will go, but will stay for only a short time."

Max nodded. "To the mountains of Saleef!"

Together, Neal, Julie, and Max righted the cart. Keeah led the pilkas to the river to drink.

Moments later, the little band was hurrying across the plains as quickly as they could. Soon they spotted sheer cliffs of rose-colored stone appearing in the dusty distance.

"Lubalunda is up there?" asked Neal. "How do we climb up those cliffs?"

"We don't!" said Max. "To the untrained eye, the entrance to Lubalunda cannot be found. That's why my old home has remained hidden for so many years. If you climb for it, you shall never find it. There is a secret way up the foothills to the peak, but you must know the road to take. And I do! So follow!"

As they galloped through the pink foothills, Keeah remembered the strange men helping Prince Ungast at the treasure fortress.

"Sparr," she said. "Ungast stole your car."

"It was a total wreck," said Neal. "Sorry."

The sorcerer's brow wrinkled. "My old car! Wreck or not, if the boy restores it, he can do much damage. That car was with me for a long time. It knows me. I am a part of it."

"We also saw three ugly creatures," Julie said. "They were tall and thin with rough skin, and they didn't speak. Ungast called them Kindus."

"I know them," said Sparr, shaking his head gravely. "Kindu warriors were special troops in Goll. They were ruthless and clever. But one thing they did better than all others."

"What?" asked Keeah.

"They are hunters," said the old sorcerer. "They have senses far more powerful than a human or even a wizard. What they seek, they find. Always."

Julie shared a look with Keeah and Neal. "They took things from the treasure fortress. A weird spiked ball. A dagger."

"And silver boots," said Neal. "I remember because they'd look really cool with my turban."

"Hold on," said Max suddenly. He stopped the cart beneath a section of rock that looked like any other. He descended, and with a wink and a nod, he pressed on the rock with both hands. *Floomp!* — it flipped around, and he was gone.

"Where'd he go?" asked Neal.

"In here!" Max called from the other side of the rock. "Come in. Come in."

The children, Galen, and Sparr pressed the rock one by one and entered . . . the tallest peak of the mountain.

The thickest, tallest trees they had ever seen grew straight up from a rolling grassy plain. The trees seemed to reach up to the very summit of the mountain, which was open to the sky.

"Behold the village of Lubalunda!" said Max.

Lubalunda was a network of tiny green houses built on the ground and in the trees and connected by bridges made of trembling spider silk.

Because Lubalunda was in the heart of the Pink Mountains of Saleef on the eastern edge of the free part of Droon, one could see from its summit nearly the whole countryside, from the Dust Hills of Panjibarrh in the south to the crest of Silversnow in the north, to the edge of the Dark Lands in the smoky east.

When a breeze blew through the trees, the village of bridges quivered with a gentle music all its own.

"Behold my home!" said Max, looking proudly at his birthplace. "It's been far too long since I've been here. I wonder if anyone remembers me —"

"Look, everyone! It's Max!" cried a voice.

Another voice called, "Max has returned!"

"I guess they do," said Keeah, smiling.

All of a sudden, the tiniest spider troll the children had ever seen swung down on a cord of spider silk. He plopped down next to them, gazing at Max in awe. "Are you . . . Uncle Maximilian?" he said.

Julie gasped. "Uncle?"

Neal gasped. "Maximilian?"

Max's eyes widened. "Are you Feodor?"

"I am!" squeaked the tiny spider troll.

Max puffed up his chest. "Yes, nephew. I am Maximilian, back after long years in the world outside. These people are the wizards Galen and Sparr, the princess Keeah, and my dear friends Julie and Neal, and we need a place to hide!"

"Come right this way!" said another little troll with bright yellow hair, bowing till his head touched the ground. "This way!"

Soon the entire village was alive with cheers of welcome.

There were many spider trolls whose hair, while standing straight up like Max's, had turned completely white. There were others who were the tiniest babies, with sprouts of orange, yellow, and even blue hair on the tops of their heads. They surrounded Max and showered him with greetings and questions.

Out marched one old spider troll with silver hair, a wide blue sash, and a badge on his jacket. He was older than the rest, and he limped through the crowd, leaning on a cane as he walked.

"Mayor Tibble!" said Max, bowing low. "I am honored."

"Welcome, all," said Mayor Tibble.

"We seek shelter," said Galen. "For now."

"And you shall have it," said Mayor Tibble. "Join me in my tree tower. It offers the best view!"

As the band of friends worked their way up to the mayor's tree tower, Keeah noticed that Galen's eyes were downcast, and he was fingering the orange cloth she'd seen before.

Something is happening, she thought. *Galen is worried. Very worried.*

As they entered the tree tower, Keeah gazed out over the Dark Lands. She sensed Gethwing's forces moving closer by the minute. Perhaps even Ungast himself was among them.

How long she and her friends would be safe was a question she could not answer.

Five

Tapestry of Evil

As the three groggles dived through swirling plumes of smoke into the Dark Lands, Prince Ungast gazed out of his balloon. Two ominous mountains of black stone lay below. Between them was a third peak, taller than the others but nearly hidden by the black fog.

"So," he said to himself, "*that's* Babblebrain?"

It wasn't.

It was Barrowbork, Gethwing's hide-out, a monstrous crag of stone that rose straight up from the ashen earth.

At its summit stood a large, flat clearing bounded by a tangled forest of rock formations that crisscrossed one another to form a menacing dome.

"How ugly," Ungast said. "In an ugly sort of way, I mean."

Ugly or not, Barrowbork was alive with activity. Funnels of black smoke and orange flame poured from a big stone furnace that stood in the clearing.

The prince knew that this was the magic forge Gethwing had told him about when they'd left Samarindo.

Ungast smiled to himself. Before long, he would be using the forge.

He pulled the balloon ropes above him and descended. Moments later, the crumpled yellow car settled with a thud near the forge. The basket landed next to it.

The three voiceless Kindu warriors who had helped him at the treasure fortress swooped down beside him. Meanwhile, a troop of plump, red-faced Ninns stumbled over. They stood staring in awe at the yellow car. They seemed to know it instantly as their former leader's.

"Bring it to the forge," Ungast said. "Time is wasting."

"Yes, Prince Ungast!" said the Ninns.

The dark prince watched the red-faced warriors unchain the crumpled wreck and haul it to a giant anvil that stood outside the furnace.

The Ninns backed away, not taking their eyes off of the car.

"It's special to you, isn't it?" said Ungast.

"It was Sparr's. I know that. He was once a pretty wicked guy, but now he's old and powerless, right?"

A low, throaty laugh came from a ledge of twisted stone coiling over the summit. Atop it sat the giant dragon himself, his wings folded behind him.

"The Ninns hold a place in their hearts for the old Sparr," Gethwing rasped. "And for his car. Which forms a part of my plan. As do you yourself, Prince Ungast."

"Me? Really?" said the prince. "You're going to have to tell me more about this plan of yours sometime."

"Oh, I shall!" said the dragon.

I bet you shall, thought Ungast. *You don't trust me, do you? Well, maybe . . . you shouldn't.*

"No matter how damaged Sparr's car may look, the Ninns are still in awe of it," said the dragon. "Do you know why?"

Ungast shrugged. "They like junk?"

"Because it contains part of the soul of its creator," said the dragon. "And once it's repaired, that soul will help you find something I need. Something only it knows how to find."

"Wow, a car with a soul," said Ungast. "It won't talk back to me, will it?"

Gethwing made that face again. "You are a funny boy," he said.

"Maybe I'm a comedian," said Ungast. "Maybe that's what I was before I became Ungast, Prince of Power."

The dragon said nothing.

Am I bothering you? the boy wondered.

But the car did interest him. He felt the power of someone's soul in it, all right, even though it didn't look like much at that moment.

Crouching on his heels, he ran his

hands over the twisted metal. Then he lay on his back and looked at it from underneath. He kicked the ragged, airless tires.

Finally, he turned to Gethwing. "I can fix it by nightfall. If no one bothers me. And you might want to find another place to roost. It's going to be hot and loud up here."

"Very well," said Gethwing, making one of those unattractive smiles. "Proceed!"

Flapping his four wings loudly, the dragon removed himself to a perch farther away.

Ungast wiggled his fingers, drew in a deep breath, and took up a hammer that lay next to the anvil.

He paused.

He could see that face everywhere, the bearded one. In wisps of smoke. In a momentary shadow. In the folds and shiftings of his mind. And the odd thing was, the more Ungast looked at the car, the more he knew exactly how to fix it. As if a voice were telling him. *Hammer here, not there. Work from below. Careful of the silver pipes.*

He tried to clear his mind. He was part of Gethwing's plan now. He'd rule an army. And he'd get a crown.

"Ungast?" said the dragon impatiently.

"I'm starting!" Using both hands, he aimed the hammer at the front bumper and swung it down with all his might.

Clank-ank-ank!

The sound bounced off the surrounding stone and buffeted the air like thunder. His arms tingled with power as the hammer struck the car. Over and over, he pounded.

Clank! Wham! Clank-ank-ank!

One hour. Two hours without stopping. Ungast battered away at the metal

unceasingly, as if possessed, smoothing, reworking, turning, hammering — all according to the vision of the vehicle in his mind. Meanwhile, Gethwing surveyed the land below with his powerful, all-seeing eyes.

"I love to view my world from on high," Gethwing said finally. "Everything is so . . ." He trailed off, then made a low, hissing noise.

Ungast stopped hammering. "What's wrong? Are you losing air, or do you see something?"

"The wizards have escaped the Ninn riders. They have vanished," Gethwing said. "I can guess where they've gone. Lubalunda."

"Loobyloony?" said Ungast.

"Lubalunda," the dragon repeated, "is the legendary village of the spider trolls, long hidden in the mountains of Saleef and nearly impossible to find."

"So?" said Ungast.

"So," said the dragon, "my plan is working. Zello's armies are scattered to the four corners of Droon. My enemies are in hiding. And the crown begins to take shape."

"What crown?" asked Ungast.

"My Crown of Wizards," said the dragon. "In my crown there are several jewels. One of the jewels is you. Another is me. The third is an old friend. Together our crown will be unbreakable."

Ungast thought of the bearded face. "Who's the old friend? Someone I know?"

"Not yet, but take a look," said Gethwing. "She is coming right now."

"Here?" said Ungast. "To Butterball?"

"Barrowbork!" Gethwing snarled.

Chuckling, Ungast set down the

hammer and leaped up to the summit. From there, he saw a tiny caravan crawling across the distant sands. At its head was a dark-haired girl in a red tunic and black boots. She was arguing with the troop of red-faced Ninns accompanying her.

"Stylish," he said. "And snotty. Is she bad?"

"Worse than bad, I hope," said the dragon. "She is Neffu, the dark side of Princess Keeah, much as you are . . . a dark prince."

Keeah? thought the boy. *She was the girl at the fortress, wasn't she? But you were going to say something else, weren't you, Gethwing? Neffu is her dark side like I am the dark side of . . . who? This Eric Hinkle kid? Is that who?*

"Neffu is a witch as powerful in her own way as the princess is in hers," said Gethwing. "With her arrival, my plan begins to weave itself together. Like a tap-estry of evil!"

A wingwolf flew to Gethwing's perch and whispered in the dragon's ear.

"Tell him to enter," said the dragon.

As the wingwolf flew off, Gethwing narrowed his eyes at Ungast. "How much longer before the car is complete?"

"It's nearly done," said Ungast, taking up the hammer again. He resumed his work.

But even as the forge's flames rose and he pounded out the last of the car's deep dents, Prince Ungast felt a chill cross the mountaintop. He turned to see a tall, face-less creature move toward him. The thing was more like fog than a man, but more like a man than a beast.

"Ungast, meet one of your new army," said the dragon. "An army of wraiths, some of the most ruthless of all magical creatures."

Ungast steeled himself to look at the space where the creature's face should have been. It was cold and blank and smooth. The wraith knelt and bowed to him. The creature was frightening, no doubt. But a part of Ungast felt proud to be its leader.

"Up, wraith," he said boldly.

Gethwing moved his claw through the air. "And there are his brothers. Your army."

The boy stepped to the edge of the summit and saw thousands upon thousands of wraiths covering the plains below.

"Are you happy now?" asked the dragon.

"I am," said Ungast. "I am."

But it was a lie.

Ungast wasn't happy.

He liked the idea of a huge army, of ruling a vast land, but every time his mind wandered, he saw faces in the dark corners of his memory. What, after all, had happened *before* the battle in Samarindo? What was his life like *before* two days ago?

His heart thudded in his chest. His eyes blurred for an instant as if he would faint. The face. The long white beard.

He stole a look at the car once more, and it finally came to him.

I know that face!

"Go, dark prince," said the dragon. "Find the treasure. Return it to me."

"I'm going," said Ungast. He pressed a green button on the dashboard.

The engine thundered to life.

Six

A Tale of Two Cities

Bzzz-flit-flit! The tiny wings of the sprite known as Flink were fluttering around Galen's head when Keeah entered the mayor's tree tower.

"No . . . no . . . it cannot be," she heard the wizard whisper to the sprite.

Flink buzzed again, and Galen paused, overlooking the long valley between Lubalunda and the smoky heights of Barrowbork. He clutched the orange fabric.

"Why now?" he said, more to himself than to Flink. He waved his hand, and the sprite disappeared.

Keeah had never seen the old wizard look so worried or so haggard.

She stepped up to him. "Galen . . ."

He whirled around to face her, stuffing his hand into his pocket. "Ah, Princess. I didn't know you were there. The news is not good. Armies are moving across Panjibarrh. The western coast is bombarded by Ninn ships. Even the Skorth, those wicked skeletons, have returned in the north. My dear . . ."

He paused as Neal, Julie, Max, and Mayor Tibble joined them. "My friends, we must take action, no matter how small and ragtag a force we are. One wants to defend every inch of our world, but we cannot. Since Ko's disappearance, Gethwing has wasted no time. Having turned Eric to his side — our poor, lost Eric! — Gethwing grows stronger by the hour. I see only one way. We must bring Eric back to us. We cannot spare any effort."

"Too bad we can't go in there and kick Gethwing right off his stinky old Bumblebee!" said Neal.

There came a call from a high tree. Feodor the spider troll cried out, "A change in the sky. Look yonder!"

All eyes turned toward the summit of the dragon's lair. The black smoke pouring up like a column of iron grew gray, then white, then vanished.

Sparr, who had been sitting on a stool in the corner of the tree tower, whispering and mumbling to himself, suddenly lifted his head. "My car. It moves. There!"

As if he could see, Sparr pointed a thin finger toward Barrowbork. Everyone turned in time to see a plume of dust race down the side of the black mountain.

"It is alive again!" said Sparr. "It takes the dark prince somewhere!"

"Maybe we shouldn't wait to find out," said Keeah. "Maybe we should follow Ungast right now. Maybe Neal has the right idea."

Neal looked at his friends. "Wait a second. I had an idea? Seriously? Who listens to me?"

"We all do, since you have become Zabilac," said Max. "First Genie of the Dove!"

Galen's hands shook. "But, Keeah, to go into the very shadow of Barrowbork? We have no army for such an effort."

"Not an army," Keeah said, "just the three of us. Julie, Neal, and me — a girl with awesome powers, a genie, and a wizard. We can follow Eric, discover

Gethwing's plan, and turn it upside down. From the inside."

"This is madness, my princess!" said Max.

Sparr laughed. "No!" he said. "This is the opposite of madness. Of all that Gethwing foresees, he will not expect you to infiltrate his lands. It sounds like the only plan to me."

"It is fraught with dangers," said Max.

Mayor Tibble nodded his gray head. "Max is correct. The Dark Lands are nothing but miles and miles of ash-covered earth, black swamps, impassable passes, and unknown dangers!"

Galen nodded. "To go far beyond the Dark Lands' border? With no help? No guide?"

"Except they *will* have a guide," said Sparr, rising to full stature. "I was in Barrowbork as a child. I know the way. I know its secret roads. We can intercept Ungast!"

The sorcerer's eyes were white and blind. His limbs were thin and weak. And yet, there was something in his face that told the children he could help.

"I may be blind," he said, "but my senses will be needed on such a journey."

Galen looked from one to another. He plunged his hand in his pocket again, and finally nodded. "For Eric, then. Find him."

Keeah's heart pounded. "Thank you," she said. "We'll be careful."

"Pack up, my friends," said Sparr. "We leave. And, sightless or not, I shall lead!"

The little band of four left the tree tower and mounted pilkas. Together they left Lubalunda and headed for the mountain trails. When they reached the foot of the Pink Mountains, a narrow fringe of green fields separated them from the clouded borders of the moon dragon's country. Dark air hung low over the vast ashen plains, while jagged peaks rose here and there in the far distance.

"Not really inviting, is it?" asked Neal.

"Not so much," said Keeah. "Come on."

No sooner had they crossed the border than they heard the flap of wings.

"Hide!" said Neal, and the little troop took shelter behind a boulder as a pack of wingwolves sailed overhead. Their gruff calls echoed to one another, and they sailed on.

"It only gets worse from here," said Sparr. "Let's move quickly. And carefully. This way."

Though he was blind, the old sorcerer's other senses were acute. Sparr guided the children past deadly swamps, bottomless pits, fields of sinking sand, and lairs of venomous snakes. Slowly but surely, they made their way across the wastes and black deserts of the outer Dark Lands.

Soon the terrain became rocky, and reluctantly they had to abandon their pilkas. The friends continued on foot, with Sparr wobbling on his cane.

"Are you sure you can do this?" Keeah asked the old sorcerer.

"Sure?" Sparr said. "Nothing is sure. But I can do nothing else. Eric must come back to us. Let's . . ."

He tilted his head and listened intently.

"Let's *what*?" asked Julie.

"Beasts!" said Sparr. "On our left!"

"Hide!" said Neal. "Again!"

They tumbled behind a ledge as a long train of lion-headed beasts galloped from the plains behind them, then vanished into a pass leading up into the black mountains.

"Onward," said the sorcerer. "Now!"

Not far ahead stood the dark rocks of the Barrowbork foothills, through which was a single passage, a narrow slice in the jagged mountains. Sparr told them it was called Sunderpass.

"Again, I have to wonder why I'm so full of ideas," Neal sighed.

"The road out of Barrowbork leads through the pass," said Sparr. "Let us surprise Ungast there. Under cover of darkness."

"Even the darkness is under cover of darkness around here," said Neal.

While Keeah held him firmly by the elbow, Sparr mumbled softly to himself, as if speaking to someone who wasn't there. Together, they climbed slowly upward toward the pass.

The sides of Sunderpass rose in sheer cliffs hundreds of feet high, but they leaned in so far that the sky — black as it was — was not even visible.

"I feel totally alone here," said Julie.

"I think that's the point," said Neal. "The Dark Lands are not a friendly place."

"Zabilac, I hear something," said Sparr. "Use your genie light to show the way."

Neal gulped. "I haven't gotten that far in the genie magic scroll yet. Hold on."

As Neal scanned the spells on his tiny scroll, Keeah stepped forward into the pass. The cliff walls came so close together, they nearly touched above her head. She slid between them and found her foot shifting on loosened ash.

Then there was a noise.

Vroom! Ooga! Ooga!

Sparr gasped. "Wait! I know that sound! It is . . . my car!"

It *was* his car. And it was gleaming and

yellow and swift as it tore through the mountain pass.

"It's totally repaired!" shouted Julie.

"As good as new?" said Sparr.

The yellow car was as good as new — as shiny and perfect as the day the sorcerer created it. Prince Ungast sat in the driver's seat. Seated next to him was Neffu, her long red scarves flying in the wind.

The car shrieked to a stop inches away from the little band.

"Well, lookee who we have here!" said Neffu. "My most favoritest cousin in the whole wide world! Princess Kee-kee!"

Keeah nearly choked. "Neffu!"

"The one and only," the dark-haired girl said. "Not counting you, of course. Because I sort of *am* you. As a witch!"

Neffu was someone Keeah had hoped never to see again, the girl she met when she struggled against her own dark side, as all wizards have to do. Neffu was Keeah's dark side just as Ungast was Eric's. The only difference was that the last time they'd met, Keeah had defeated her dark side, and Neffu had vanished.

But not, apparently, forever.

"What are *you* doing here?" said Keeah. "I thought I sent you away."

"And I told you I'd be back," snarled Neffu. "I've been waiting a long time since you sent me to the Underworld. I really didn't care for it there."

"Why not?" said Julie. "The fires there must bring out the color of your eyes."

Neffu's eyes flashed red at Julie. "I've learned a thing or two since you shuttled me off last time. This time, I'm here to stay. Gethwing's going to make me a star. In fact, Ungie and I are on a mission."

"What is your mission?" said Sparr, speaking directly to Prince Ungast.

The dark prince said nothing.

Keeah watched the boy in purple. Ungast didn't speak, but searched their faces one by one, as if looking for something or someone. He narrowed his eyes at Lord Sparr.

Eric? said Keeah silently.

There was no change in his expression.

Neffu whipped her scarves behind her. "But enough talk. We've got a mission and I'm here to stop you cold. So bundle up."

The dark princess waved her hands, and a great black cloud appeared over the friends. Icicles began to fall on them like daggers.

"Remember these?" Neffu said with a laugh. "No poison this time, but they're still plenty painful!"

"I'll find a spell against this," said Neal, frantically searching his tiny scroll.

Neffu laughed. "That's an awfully big turban for an awfully small boy!"

She hurled a giant icicle right at Neal. *Clong!* It slammed the cliff over his head and buried him in a mound of ice chips.

"Now, if you'll excuse us," said Neffu, "we've got to go. Stay warm. Or not! Step on it, Ungie."

The prince focused his eyes as if he were waking from a dream. Then he slammed his foot on the gas and — *vroom!* — the car tore around them and away through the pass.

As it did, the air above the children flashed silver, and more giant bolts of ice rained down on them.

Seven

Sunken Treasure

Crash! Blam! Crack!

The children dived to the ground and rolled to the sides of the pass as the ice bolts blasted at them.

Anxious to protect the old sorcerer from the deadly icicles, Keeah pulled Sparr close and huddled over him.

"What now, Zabilac?" cried Julie.

Neal crawled over to her. "Uh . . . I just saw a spell against big ice thingies," he said, still hunting through his scroll. "It's in here somewhere, but you can't bookmark a scroll!"

Finally, Neal found the charm. "Got it! Everyone ready?"

"We've *been* ready," said Keeah.

"Chebba-bebba-root-snoot!"

Wha-poom! The storm vanished as quickly as it had appeared.

"Good thing genie magic is as old as Goll magic," said Neal.

"Good thing you found that charm," said Julie, shaking the ice chips off of herself.

Keeah helped Sparr to his feet. "I never wanted to see Neffu again," she said. "My opposite, a witch with as much power as I have. She fooled me."

"She fooled all of us," said Sparr. "I did not sense her coming. All I sensed was my car. This is my fault."

"No, it's Gethwing's fault," said Keeah. "Bringing Neffu and Ungast together? It's worse than my worst nightmares. We need some way to follow them."

Sparr bowed his head. "Perhaps now I can prove helpful. When I was young . . . and before I had my car . . . I used to . . ." He trailed off, took a deep breath, and went still.

All at once, the ashes under their feet began to shift around and take shape. Soon, they formed what looked like a small cart with runners instead of wheels.

"A sand sled!" said Keeah. "I remember these! My father made me one when I was small. I loved it."

"Then hop on, and follow that car!" said Sparr. "All aboard!"

The little band jumped into the sled and shot unseen after the yellow car.

The sand of the black deserts was shiny and smooth as they raced quickly over the long miles.

Afternoon wore on. And still they followed.

Swarms of wingwolves darkened the sky, but the children focused only on the car bouncing over dunes and splashing through low-lying swamps on its many fat tires.

After several hours, the yellow car approached the southern coast and began to slow. Black waves crashed against the shore.

"The Serpent Sea!" said Sparr. "What are they after, I wonder? Let us move closer."

"And listen in to what they're saying," said Neal. He stretched his turban to cover them all, and they soon heard the conversation between Ungast and Neffu.

"I'm going to have lots of fun with this car," said Ungast.

Neffu snorted. "It's okay. But when I become an official dark princess, you know what I want? A big crown."

"I want a *huge* crown," said Ungast.

"Crown, did he say?" whispered Sparr.

Neffu shook her head. "Well, my crown is even bigger than yours. It's gold and has diamonds all over it."

"Mine is actually *made* of diamonds," said Ungast. "And it has nuggets of gold on it!"

"So does mine. Plus, it's magical."

"And I have a magical cape that flies by itself —"

"I have two capes," said Neffu.

"And matching boots," said Ungast.

"Fine, but I have matching monsters."

Ungast turned to her. "Matching monsters? What does that even mean?"

Neffu shrugged. "I don't know. But I have a hundred of them. I mean, a thousand."

"Maybe, but pretty much all they do is carry *my* big monsters around," said Ungast.

Neal rolled his eyes. "This has got to be the dumbest evil conversation I've ever eavesdropped on!"

"Those spoiled brats!" Julie growled.

"Hush," said Keeah. "Look."

The dark prince and princess suddenly stopped speaking and looked out to sea. There in the black water stood the distant island of Kahfoo, a rocky promontory in the shape of a giant snake's head.

"That's the landmark Gethwing told us to look for," said Neffu. "Phase two begins!"

All at once — *vrrrt!* — a glass dome slid

over the cockpit, and the car picked up speed.

"What's going on?" asked Sparr. "Tell me."

"He's speeding up," said Keeah, pressing forward, urging the sled to go faster.

"They're going into the water!" cried Julie.

With a burst of speed, the yellow car shot straight out to sea and vanished under the waves with a tremendous splash.

The sled slid to a stop on the black beach.

"Holy cow!" said Neal. "They've disappeared!"

Sparr paced nervously. "I worry about what they are doing. We must know."

"I'll fly out there," said Julie. In a flash, she was in the air, circling the spot where the car had disappeared. Then she returned to the beach. "There's nothing there. The car just . . . vanished."

"No," said Sparr. "No . . . no . . ."

The expression on Sparr's face reminded Keeah of the way Galen had looked in the tree tower back in Lubalunda.

What is going on? she wondered.

"The *Jaffa Wind*," she said. "I'll call Nelag to bring the ship. We can sail out there."

Nelag, she said silently, ***we're near Kahfoo. Come at once! We need you!***

Before long, the blue sails of the *Jaffa Wind* swept into view. At the wheel sat Nelag the pretend wizard. Within minutes, the three children and Sparr were onboard. Soon they were over the spot where the yellow car had disappeared.

"What do you think he's after down there?" asked Neal, peering into the water.

"No matter," said Nelag, scratching his ears. "You won't see him again. Not even right . . . now!"

All of a sudden — *whooooom!* — the surface of the water exploded, and the yellow car shot straight up and soared away.

"Look there!" said Julie.

The children could just make out something lying in the backseat of the yellow car — a treasure chest made of black iron with gold chains locking it shut.

"What's in that strongbox?" asked Neal. "Lord Sparr, do you know?"

Though he could not see, Sparr traced the movements of the car in the sky. "I dare not guess!"

"There will be no stopping us now!" cried Neffu. "Gethwing will rule . . . everything!"

Eight

Taking Sides

"Follow that car!" said Neal.

"The *Jaffa Wind* doesn't do much," said Nelag, "but it flies very well!"

"Which, of course, it doesn't," said Keeah. "But I just remembered something. Nelag, is the storage chest still in my cabin?"

"Absolutely not," the pretend wizard said.

"Good!" said Keeah. "I need something from it."

The princess ran belowdecks and came back up a moment later holding a rolled-up carpet. She flapped it open on the deck.

"This is an official Pasha carpet I used to keep for emergencies," she said. "And this is definitely an emergency. Everyone on!"

As Keeah and the others carefully helped the hobbling old sorcerer onto the carpet, she wondered how much Sparr really knew of what was happening. The sorcerer's magic was nearly gone. He was blind. He had aged so much in the last few weeks that he seemed ready to collapse. She felt sorry for him. But she knew they needed him.

Seconds later, the carpet swept through the sky after the yellow car.

"We need to stop Gethwing from using whatever is in that chest," said Sparr. "I fear it's some old magic that has lain hidden on the ocean's floor for ages. We cannot risk Gethwing getting his claws on it!"

"His creepy, ugly claws," said Neal.

"Well said," Sparr agreed.

Keeah urged the carpet faster and faster, and soon it pulled up behind the yellow car. Neffu turned. "Well, look who's trying to pass us. Lose them, Ungie."

Ungast swung his head around and saw them. He narrowed his eyes at Sparr. His mouth dropped open. "You —"

With a swift turn of the wheel, the dark prince plunged the car downward. As it dipped and slowed, the carpet shot above it, and Ungast flipped over and swooped up behind them.

"I like this view better," said Neffu. "Prepare for an ice storm, kiddies!"

"What, that again?" said Neal. "Don't you have anything new to offer?"

Neffu narrowed her eyes at him. "All right. How about — birdies?"

"That's fine. We love birdies!" scoffed Julie.

Neffu's fingers twitched and flicked. Suddenly, a flock of birds appeared. Giant black birds. With clawed feet and long, jagged beaks and great leathery wings. At Neffu's command, the birds swarmed the little carpet.

"Except we don't love *those* birdies!" cried Neal. "Dive!"

As Neal and Julie did their best to swat the birds away, Keeah steered the carpet down, then banked sharply, pulling alongside the car. She steadied it, then leaped out, grabbing on to the spare tire behind Ungast.

"Hey, no extra passengers," snapped Neffu. "You're gonna pay for this ride!"

The snotty witch had just raised her hands to blast at the princess when Ungast turned the wheel abruptly to avoid hitting a giant black bird. The quick movement threw Neffu across the seat, and her shot went wild, exploding near the birds and scaring them off.

"Hey, whose side are you on!" Neffu snapped.

"The side that wins!" said the prince, giving Keeah a hard stare. "Finish her off!"

At that moment, Keeah saw in Ungast's face something that reminded her of Eric. She snatched at the treasure chest, but Neffu knocked her hands away from it.

"Eric!" Keeah shouted. "You will come back to us. I'll make sure of it."

"Whatev," snarled the prince.

"You will!" she said. "You can't stop the future —"

"Blah-blah," snapped Neffu. "How about you just land that carpet? In Gethwing's lair!"

"No, thanks," called Neal. "Beaglebutt is *your* hideout!"

"Ha! You mean Blunderbuss!" Ungast shouted.

For an instant, Keeah saw a trace of a smile on Ungast's lips.

"Really?" said Neal. "And all this time I thought it was Bubblebath!"

"Cut it out, you two!" said Neffu.

As Keeah reached for the treasure chest once more, Ungast shouted, "Get away from that!" He twisted the wheel violently, and Keeah fell back onto the carpet.

In a moment she would remember forever, Keeah saw Sparr struggle to his feet and leap — twenty feet! — through the air and into the car.

"Sparr!" Keeah gasped.

"No!" cried Neffu.

Sparr fell into the seat next to her and grabbed the chest. Without pausing, he flung the chest onto the carpet.

Neffu cried out and dived after it. She landed hard on the carpet, next to Julie and Neal.

Before Keeah, Julie, or Neal could react, the witch had stolen the treasure away again. Grasping it tightly to her chest, she stepped off the carpet into empty air.

"Birds!" she cried. The giant black birds swept under her and bore her up, still clinging to the treasure chest.

As the car soared into the sky, Ungast and Sparr grappled with each other. The old sorcerer tried to get control of the steering wheel, but he was no match for

the young prince. The car zoomed away toward Barrowbork. Neffu and the birds followed it, leaving the carpet far behind.

"Oh, my gosh!" said Julie. "Sparr is gone! Ungast has him!"

By then it was too late to chase them. A pack of wingwolves joined the car, and they vanished into the smoke-filled skies over Barrowbork.

"This is terrible!" Keeah cried. Her heart quaked. No good could possibly come of the old sorcerer being Gethwing's captive.

Julie righted the carpet. "We have to return to Lubalunda. We have to tell Galen!"

The three friends raced across the skies toward the Saleef mountains. They circled once and spotted Max and Galen in the mayor's tree tower. Max was perched at the highest lookout, scanning the landscape. He waved to them, and they descended.

Keeah was the first to notice Galen's grim expression. "What's wrong? What has happened?"

"Lumpland," said Max, wiping tears from his cheeks. "Lumpland has fallen to the wingwolves. King Khan has led the Lumpies into hiding. The wraiths attacked the Orkin homeland. Our blue-faced friends have fled, too."

"Five times we have tried to meet up with Zello's armies," said Galen. "And five times, we have been driven back. We are besieged!"

Max nodded. "Tell us what you have seen."

The children told them everything.

Galen mumbled under his breath when he heard of the loss of Sparr and again when he was told of the sunken chest. "Magic treasure often contains the darkest forces," he said. "Gethwing grows in power. Ancient and new. And now Sparr is lost to us." The wizard's face was ashen with worry.

Suddenly, Max stiffened. "Something moved down there. I saw it."

The children crowded up the ladder to the highest lookout post. They saw a flicker of light on the plains below the Saleef mountains. It vanished. Another flicker, closer this time. And again. Again.

"Gethwing's armies are coming," Keeah said. "We're not safe here anymore."

"Coming?" said Max. "To the spider trolls' home? But we have never . . . oh, dear!"

"So Gethwing's forces have tightened their web around us, cutting us off from the rest of Droon," said Galen. "Wingwolves have clouded the sky. The moon dragon's wraiths have darkened the land. Beast forces have united under the banner of ancient Goll. Zello's armies are far away. A web of evil surrounds us, a web of power and cunning —"

"Ahem!" said a voice.

Everyone turned to see Mayor Tibble, his silver hair standing straight up from his wrinkly forehead.

"A web, is it?" he said. "Perhaps you forget the best websmen in the world? Spider trolls! Webs cannot harm us. Webs can help us prevail!"

Galen paused, his eyes wide. "So, my valiant friend. You have a plan?"

Tibble smiled. "I certainly do!"

"They're coming now!" cried Max, peering below. "Gethwing's forces are coming! Lubalunda is being attacked! To arms!"

Nine

The Battle of Lubalunda

The mayor quickly issued orders to his people, while Galen took command of the children and helped prepare the village for attack.

No sooner had the walls been made secure than the call came. "Ninns! At the base of the foothills. Thousands of them!"

"They shall not enter the perimeter of our village," called Mayor Tibble.

But his rallying cry was answered from below by the shouting of Ninns.

"Charge!" they boomed. "Up the Pink Mountains! Batter down the secret door! Take the spider troll village!"

As the children raced forward to defend the secret entrance, the trees beyond the summit were alive with the sound of slithering snakes.

Only they weren't snakes.

They were wraiths!

And at their head was none other than Prince Ungast himself. "Charge!" he cried.

As noisy as the Ninn warriors were — huffing and stumbling up the mountainsides, their weapons clattering — the wraiths were as silent as sleep, surrounding the village quickly and quietly. The air grew icy cold as they advanced.

Using wands that glowed with purple

light, the wraith warriors froze the little trolls where they stood.

"Defend Lubalunda!" Max shouted from below.

"You shall not enter the city!" shouted the mayor. "You will not come an inch closer —"

A passing wraith touched his shoulder with a glowing wand and slithered on. Little, silver-haired Tibble froze in mid-yell, his mouth open, his hands raised in tiny fists.

"Stop them in the trees!" yelled Julie.

Keeah ran to the tower. "Galen, we need your magic at the village entrance. The Ninns are battering the outside walls —"

She stopped.

Galen, his forehead wet with perspiration, his cloak ragged from the first attack of wraiths, nodded his weary head. In his hand was the orange fabric. It was nearly worn through.

"The time is wrong. I am needed here. Why take me away?" he whispered to himself.

"Galen, what is that?" Keeah asked. "Who are you talking to?"

At the same time, an explosion rang through the village. It came from the secret entrance.

"Galen! The door!" Keeah cried.

The old wizard threw the fabric to the floor of the tree tower and took Keeah's arm. "Come with me! Now!"

The two wizards flew down from the tower straight to the secret entrance just as a troop of Ninns burst through the rock and into the village.

"You shall not pass!" boomed the wizard.

Flang! Clonk! Galen swung his mighty staff up and down as if he were drawing on the air. The troop of attacking Ninns toppled into itself and fell back outside the door.

"Seal up the doorway!" Keeah cried.

Together the two wizards sent a beam of brilliant light at the broken entrance and sealed it shut.

But the number of attackers was far too many for the small band of defenders. With another explosion, the Ninns burst through again.

"Fall back!" Galen shouted, retreating to the safety of a ledge on the inside of the hollow peak. "Fall back to the tree house!"

The children, Max, and Galen were soon safely inside the tree tower. When they looked down, they saw the hillsides below moving with thousands of Ninns and wraith warriors. The wraiths slithered up the crags while the Ninns clambered up the pink stone to the summit.

The old wizard's features were drawn and worried. "Gethwing's power is nearly complete."

Keeah searched Galen's face. What if . . . what if this war proved too much for him?

"What can we do?" she asked. "We have to do something now."

While the battle raged below, Galen paced and nodded, paused, nodded, and paced again. He scanned the trees, looked at the sky, stroked his beard.

Suddenly, he smiled. "This reminds me of a time, oh, long ago. . . ." He drifted off.

"Galen?" whispered Keeah.

The wizard started, as if woken from a deep sleep. He turned to the children. "What can we do? Together, perhaps not much. We don't have the strength to defeat Gethwing's armies. But separately? Separately we may hold the key. While Max and I do our best here, you must go to the Upper World."

"The Upper World?" said Neal in surprise. "Aren't we needed here? Why should we go there?"

Galen released a long breath. "I am learning, hour by hour, moment by moment, that the prophecy of Emperor Ko is coming true, regardless of Eric's accidental wounding. Go to Eric's home. To Eric's home . . ." He drifted off again.

"What do you want us to do?" asked Julie.

Galen blinked at something on the floor. He picked up the orange fabric, which lay at his feet.

"Ah, yes," he said. "Go to Eric's home and discover if his mother knows a secret about him. She may not realize how important what she knows is. Tell her what happened to Eric. Tell her everything, if you must. She may be our only hope of saving him. There must be a secret from his past. . . ."

"Like the Pearl Sea?" said Neal.

The wizard nodded. "Like the Pearl Sea."

Keeah breathed deeply. "If we can't battle Gethwing, we have to bring Eric back to our side. If this quest has any chance of helping him, we have to go. Now!"

"Then go," said Galen, scanning the countryside below. "And our blessing be with you. I will remain here and try to keep Lubalunda free."

With a quick move of his hand, Galen sprayed sparkly dust into the air. It caught the light like silver rain, then fell lightly to the ground. When it did, the shape of steps shimmered before them, and the rainbow stairs appeared.

Galen gave the pouch to Keeah. "Ah, well, I can still do this, it seems," he said. "The stairs will bring you back exactly where you need to be. Now go. And may all good things go with you."

With that, he began to pace the tree tower once more.

Keeah, Neal, and Julie looked at one another. Without a word, they raced up the glittering stairs to the Upper World.

Ten

The Impossible Riddle

With a brief look back at the dark forces swarming the spider troll homeland, Keeah, Julie, and Neal rushed up the rainbow stairs.

Although they hadn't thought for a long time about the strange jewel known as the Pearl Sea, they knew its story by heart.

One of the most powerful objects in either world was the wondrous Moon

Medallion created by Zara, Queen of Light, mother of Galen, Sparr, and Urik.

The Medallion was an encyclopedia of ancient knowledge, a device of untold power, and the artifact that united the wizardry of Zara's magic dynasty.

But the real strength of the object came from the parts created by each of her sons.

Galen fashioned the Ring of Midnight, which circled the Medallion.

Sparr made the Twilight Star, which twirled within the Ring.

And Urik created the Pearl Sea, which glowed from its center.

When all three parts fit into the Medallion, completing it, it became a device of immense power unmatched by any other.

Urik had long been lost in time and so was his Pearl Sea. Until one day, Gethwing invaded the Upper World seeking it, and the Pearl turned up.

In Eric Hinkle's house.

How had it come to be there? When had it arrived? And why was the Pearl hidden there, of all places?

These were the mysteries that the children needed to answer now.

They scrambled up the last few steps and into the closet of Eric's basement.

While they were in Droon, no time had passed in the Upper World. Mrs. Hinkle was still knocking on the closet door, just as they had known she would be.

"Eric? Eric!"

Keeah closed her eyes and murmured the words she had spoken earlier that day and — *zing!* — she looked just like Eric.

Neal removed his turban, folded it into his pocket, and put his hand on the doorknob. **Ready?** he asked silently.

Ready, said Julie.

The three friends each took a deep breath, then opened the closet door and stepped out into the basement.

Mrs. Hinkle stood there, clutching the kids' soccer ball. She stared at Neal and Julie, then looked Keeah up and down.

"Hi . . . Mom," said the princess.

Eric's mother shook her head, slowly at first, then more rapidly. "You're not Eric. You're not him. Where is my son?"

Keeah's heart thundered. "Uh . . ."

Neal gulped. "No, seriously, this is Eric," he said. "Really. Hey, Eric, tell your mom about the reason you got detention in math class. Only the real Eric knows that."

"Uh . . . right . . . detention," said Keeah. *What's detention?*

Mrs. Hinkle gazed at each of the children in turn, then shook her head again. "I saw this ball fly all by itself. And I know my son. You aren't Eric. Where is he? What happened to him?"

Seeing from Mrs. Hinkle's face that they shouldn't — couldn't — lie to her anymore, Keeah snapped her fingers. Instantly, her long blond hair returned, her T-shirt and jeans became her usual blue tunic, and the glasses vanished from her nose.

Mrs. Hinkle dropped the soccer ball. "Oh . . . my . . . How did . . . Was that . . . magic?"

She slumped into an old stuffed chair near the workbench.

"We'll tell you the truth," said Julie.

And they did.

In fact, they told her everything from the beginning. They told the whole saga of Droon, from the day Julie, Neal, and Eric first discovered the staircase to Droon to the time Eric was wounded by Emperor

Ko's magical ice dagger to the moment Eric battled his dark side in the City of Dreams and only Prince Ungast emerged from the wreckage.

"I . . . I . . ." Mrs. Hinkle started. She couldn't go on.

"It's hard to understand, we know," said Neal. "Sometimes we don't even believe it ourselves."

"But there *can't* be a whole other world . . . down there!" Eric's mother said.

"There is, and I'm princess there," said Keeah, "at least until the beasts take over. That's why we're here."

"But I need Eric to come home!" Mrs. Hinkle cried.

"We do, too," said Neal. "We're in trouble without him. We need him to come back."

"But is he . . . gone?" Eric's mother asked.

"No," said Keeah, her eyes welling up. "He's not gone. Not really. But he's trapped and in danger. We need to find something, anything, maybe a secret that only you and Eric know, that will help draw him out from the prison of Prince Ungast. Droon will fall if we don't."

Mrs. Hinkle listened to the princess. Then, without a word, she left the basement and hurried straight upstairs to the second floor.

The children followed her into her bedroom closet and watched as she took a small wooden chest down from a high shelf.

She opened the chest and frowned.

"It's empty. I was going to show you something. It's the only secret I know," she said, "but it's gone."

"The Pearl?" said Keeah.

Mrs. Hinkle turned to her. "How did you know that?"

"Because I was here when Eric found it," Keeah said.

"Then what happened to it?" Mrs. Hinkle asked.

"We told you about Gethwing," said Julie. "Eric found the Pearl when the moon dragon came to your town. Gethwing wanted it."

"And he nearly had it," said Neal, "except that Eric kept it safe. The question is, If a wizard made the Pearl, how did it end up here?"

Mrs. Hinkle looked at the children for a long moment. "I can't answer that. All I know is . . . this."

She lifted the velvet lining of the chest and pulled out a brown envelope. She opened it and slid out an old photograph. It showed a man wearing a white hat. He was standing next to an old airplane with curved wings.

"This is my great-great-grandfather," Mrs. Hinkle said. "He was a flyer. This was his blue plane."

The children studied the picture. Julie and Neal remembered the man from the time Eric had done a school report on his ancestors.

On the back was the date: *Summer 1909.*

"Did Eric ever meet him?" asked Keeah.

Mrs. Hinkle shook her head. "No. He passed away long before Eric was born. But something happened once when Eric was very young. It was early one morning. It was fall. There were leaves on the ground. I was up here. I heard crying outside. I looked out this window and saw Eric — little, golden-haired Eric — stuck up in a tree. High up in the top branches. It was that tree."

She pointed to one of the three apple trees by the side of the house. "By the time I ran downstairs to help him . . ."

She drifted off to silence.

"Yes?" said Keeah. "By the time you got there?"

Mrs. Hinkle flinched as if she had forgotten Keeah, Julie, and Neal were there. "Eric was back on the ground. Unhurt. Standing there as if by . . . magic."

The children looked at one another.

"Did he say how he got down?" asked Julie.

Mrs. Hinkle shook her head. "I asked him. But he couldn't speak. Maybe he was afraid. Or surprised. Or shocked. When he opened his hand, he held a big pearl in it. It was so beautiful. Later he told me an old man in a white hat gave it to him. He described him to me. It sounded exactly like my great-great-grandfather. I knew it couldn't be him because he had passed away long ago, but when I showed Eric this picture, he got very excited. 'That's him!' he said over and over. I told him as gently as I could that it wasn't possible."

"What did Eric say?" asked Neal.

Mrs. Hinkle fingered the photograph. "He just cried and cried. Over the next few days, I tried to talk to him about what had happened, but he said he didn't remember any of it.

"But, really, it *wasn't* possible. I visited my great-great-grandfather's grave when I was a girl. He was a very early aviator."

Mrs. Hinkle paused and looked at Julie, Neal, and Keeah in turn. "The Pearl is gone now. Will Eric come back?"

Keeah felt her chest heave. "Y-yes," she said. "I promise you. We love Eric.

We need him. Like you do. We will find him."

Should we make her forget all of this? Julie asked silently.

Keeah nodded. ***We have to***.

"I think this photo might be what you need," said Mrs. Hinkle. "Maybe Eric — or that other boy — will remember it. Keeah, you give it to him."

"Me?"

Eric's mother nodded, placing it in Keeah's hands. "Something tells me you'll know what to do. You're special to Eric, aren't you?"

Neal and Julie looked at Keeah.

The princess felt her heart ready to burst. She knew then that nothing would stop her from bringing Eric back to them. And to his mother.

"I think I am," said the princess. "As special as he is to me."

Then Mrs. Hinkle began to cry. "Oh, dear, what am I going to tell Eric's father?"

"You don't have to say anything," said Keeah, holding the woman's hand. "You won't remember this. If everything goes well, Eric will be back home tonight."

The princess couldn't imagine what she and her friends would have to do to make that happen. She could hardly believe she'd even spoken the words. But Mrs. Hinkle nodded slowly, as if she wanted to believe it really would happen. And that was enough.

"We'll do everything we can," said Neal.

"We're sorry to do this," said Julie.

Mrs. Hinkle nodded. "Of course, dears. Do what you have to. Do *everything* you have to, to bring my son back."

Keeah spoke several soft words over Mrs. Hinkle and murmured some to herself.

As the princess became Eric's look-alike once more, his mother's tears dried and her face brightened.

"Oh!" she said. "What am I doing here? I need to go to the cheese shop!"

Neal sighed. "What I wouldn't give for some Swiss with lots of holes in it. I'm so hungry —"

"Your brain has lots of holes in it," said Julie. "Come on!"

The friends charged down the stairs to the basement closet.

Keeah wondered how she would use the photograph to bring Eric back, but she slipped it carefully into the pouch Galen had given her, determined to find a way.

Julie turned off the closet light. In a flash — *whoosh!* — the rainbow stairs appeared, and the three friends raced down the shimmering steps to Droon.

In the distance, they saw the tree tower of Lubalunda.

And they froze in shock.

A black banner flew over the spider troll village. It depicted the horned head of Gethwing.

"No . . . no!" cried Keeah. "Galen! Max! What happened?"

"Guys, I hate to say this," said Neal. "But I think Galen's on his own this time. Look."

Below them they saw hordes of beasts gathering at the foot of Barrowbork. They were making their way to the summit.

"We have to save Eric," said Julie.

Keeah jumped down two steps at a time. "And we have to hurry!"

Eleven

The Jewels in the Crown

Hot, dark rain was falling by the time Keeah, Neal, and Julie stepped off the bottom stair at the foot of the black peak of Barrowbork.

Thumping and grunting sounded behind them.

"Hide!" whispered Neal. "For, like, the fifth time today!"

The three friends dived behind a

broken column as a squad of lion-headed beasts galloped past. They entered a narrow pass leading to the summit and disappeared.

Looking back once more at Lubalunda, Keeah took a deep breath. "I'm sure Galen has everyone safe. Our work is here."

"It's going to be a lot of work, too, staying clear of the beasts," said Neal.

"Invisibility fog will help," said the princess. "But we're in the heart of the Dark Lands now, so it may not last long."

She conjured a small cloud to cover them.

"Up we go," said Julie.

And up they went. It took the children four solid hours to make their way up the jagged rocks. Twice, they had to halt where they were so as not to become trapped by packs of roaming wraiths.

When the kids finally reached the summit, the invisibility fog was nearly gone. They took cover among the rocks circling the clearing.

What they saw sent icy shivers through them.

Black banners flew from the rocks above, cauldrons spurted sizzling green flames, and multiple stairways led to a platform on which sat a giant black throne surrounded by hundreds of faceless wraiths. Gethwing himself sat on the throne, his fiery eyes fixed downward.

Keeah knew she would have to dig deep into her magic to find the power to battle Gethwing and Neffu. But what sort of magic could she use both to stop Ungast and not harm Eric? And how would she get him to see the photograph?

"Down there," whispered Julie. "I see a place. Quickly, before we're spotted."

Together, the three friends picked their way down among the coiled stones to a hidden place behind the throne, where they made themselves small and listened.

Ten wraiths marched up to the throne in formation and stood at attention. One raised a large club and struck a gong on the side of the throne. It reverberated for a few moments, then the summit went silent.

Gethwing raised his head slowly and got up from his throne. Over his dark dragon scales, he wore thick plates of black war armor that glinted in the torchlight.

"Ungast!" boomed the dragon. "Bring forth the treasure!"

"I will," the boy said. "But you know, Gethwing, I've been thinking."

"Oh, have you?" said the dragon.

"Yes. You see, I was driving along,

minding my own business, when all of a sudden, I picked up a passenger. And I'm thinking maybe you want a fourth jewel in that crown of yours. One you can get for cheap. What do you say?"

"Who is it?" asked the dragon.

Ungast snapped his fingers, and the three Kindu warriors brought Lord Sparr into the clearing. The old sorcerer was bound in chains from head to toe.

"No! No!" whispered Keeah.

Gethwing stared and stared. Slowly, he began to nod his massive head. "A fourth jewel for my crown! Yes! What other surprises do you have for me?"

"A big one," said Ungast.

A troop of Ninns ushered Galen himself into the clearing. He was not bound. But his hair was disheveled, his robes ripped, his eyes blank.

"Oh!" Julie gasped.

The wizard stumbled from one rock to another, looking from face to face without recognition.

"What happened to the old man?" asked the dragon.

Ungast drew in a breath and let it out. "He claims that someone is coming for him. Anusa the genie. He says she has called and he must go with her. He won't be a threat to us anymore."

The three children were stunned.

The old wizard. Their great friend. The First Wizard of Droon. Going away? Gone!

While they watched, Galen sank lower and lower into himself, his white beard hanging to his knees. He kept up a steady murmur to himself. "Oh . . . oh . . . oh . . ."

"Any other surprises for me?" Gethwing asked Ungast.

The dark prince smirked. "Aren't these

two enough for you? Gosh, you're hard to please."

Gethwing ignored his impudence. Waving one enormous claw, the moon dragon called forth a procession of Ninns. They marched in, bringing the black chest the children had seen earlier in the back of Sparr's car. The red-faced soldiers bowed before the throne and set the chest on the ground.

"Open it," said Gethwing.

The Ninns fumbled with the chains for a moment. When the lid finally flew up, a golden glow flashed over the throne, illuminating the dragon's terrifying features.

Though blind, Sparr seemed to feel the glow upon his face, too. He stepped forward as if to "see" the light, then he began to tremble.

"What is the treasure?" Neal whispered.

"Whatever it is, Sparr recognizes it," said Keeah.

Gethwing raised his massive arms. "Months lost at the bottom of the Serpent Sea have done nothing to diminish your beauty . . . or your power! Bring it to me!"

"Talk about nice trinkets," said Neffu, her fingers reaching for it.

Prince Ungast swatted Neffu's hands away. "I'll do it," he said. Thrusting both hands into the chest, the boy who used to be Eric Hinkle took hold of the object and held it high.

Sparr fell to his knees with a wail. "No!"

"My gosh, no!" whispered Julie, bracing herself to keep from falling. "I can't believe it!"

What the dark prince held in his hand was a coiled band of gold in the shape of a snake. It was circled upon itself, its head arched up in attack. It gleamed in its own brilliant light.

The children knew exactly what it was.

"The Coiled Viper!" whispered Keeah, shaking all over. "Ungast found the Coiled Viper!"

The Viper was the most powerful of Lord Sparr's Three Powers. It was what brought the beast emperor Ko back to life after four hundred years of charmed sleep. It was what turned Sparr into a young boy. It was what turned him back into a man again. It was what had the power to rule Droon.

Most of all, Keeah knew the dark magic the Coiled Viper was capable of. The Viper had been lost at sea when Sparr escaped a vicious attack by Ko and Gethwing. And now it had been recovered.

All at once, Gethwing's plan was clear.

The moon dragon would wear the crown and bind all the dark armies to himself in a way not even Ko had done. Gethwing would conquer Droon as none had been able to do in the past. And Droon as the children knew it would cease to be.

Lord Sparr raised his old head and turned it this way and that, unseeing, but — Keeah knew — sensing everything.

Including her and her friends.

The sorcerer shook. "No . . . no. The Viper should never have been dredged up from the bottom of that black sea. Let me go in peace. I am frail. I am too old to play these games!"

"No games," said Gethwing. "We are playing for real. I — we — want you to join our dynasty. And you shall!"

With that, Gethwing took the Coiled Viper into his claws and lifted it over his head.

"And now we see what the Coiled Viper can do! Create the circle of power I have always dreamed of!"

"No!" cried Keeah. "You won't use it!"

She jumped from the peak above and landed between Sparr and the moon dragon. Neal and Julie raced to her side.

Ninns quickly surrounded them, but Keeah broke free, rushing at Ungast and crying, "Eric, come back to us!"

Ungast pushed her away, but Keeah struggled to stay near him and managed to slip the photograph inside his cloak.

"You can't use the Viper!" she said.

"But we will," said Ungast, as a pair of wraiths trapped Keeah from behind in their iron grip. He looked at the princess closely. "You can't stop the future."

Keeah stared at him. "But . . ."

"Silence!" boomed Gethwing. "The world changes now!"

Holding the Viper directly over him, Gethwing lowered it onto his spiked head. The moment he did, beams of purple light shot from the Viper's jeweled eyes. The beams slithered through the air like a pair of hissing snakes before striking Lord Sparr's blind eyes.

The sorcerer rose to his feet, then floated above the ground.

"I have waited centuries for this moment!" shouted the moon dragon. "Behold the power of my Viper. Behold the future of Droon!"

The wraiths stood motionless, the Kindu stood motionless, but the Ninns quaked to see the Viper's fierce light fall upon their old leader.

And then, with awe on their faces, the Ninns knelt and bowed to the ground.

"Lord Sparr!" they cried.

Twelve

What's to Become of the Boy?

The Ninns bowed low, touching their foreheads on the rocky ground as the figure of the blind old sorcerer began to change.

Sparr tried to shield his face from the heat and light of the purple beam shooting from the eyes of the Coiled Viper.

Keeah tried with all her might to make Ungast look into his pocket, yet she knew her powers were almost worthless so deep in the Dark Lands. With her last ounce of magic, she sent a spark at the prince. It fizzled as it struck his cloak.

"You sure you wanna do all this?" asked Neffu. "I mean, why waste the Viper on an old guy like him? Droon belongs to the young. Like me! And Ungast, I guess. What do you think, Ungie?"

The prince pulled his cloak more tightly around him and paused, turning away for a moment.

When he turned back, he glanced at Neffu. "If not for Lord Sparr, Droon wouldn't be half as evil as it is. Oooh. Look now!"

The chains binding the sorcerer burst apart, and his ragged robes swirled in a wind that seemed to blow around only him. His dark cloak lengthened as he grew taller. A spiked helmet appeared to grow out of his head. His white hair darkened and turned a deep, rich black.

Suddenly, Sparr clasped his hands over his ears as if in pain, but when he drew them away, a black fin, edged in purple, jutted out behind each ear.

In a moment, it was over.

Sparr was standing firmly on his feet amid the silence of the summit. With a grin forming on his lips as it had not in a very long time, Lord Sparr stretched his neck, cracked his knuckles, and peered at his reflection in Gethwing's shiny armor.

"Oh . . . yes!" he said. "I've missed me, but I'm back and I'm beautiful!"

"Sparr, no —" said Keeah.

"No?" snapped the sorcerer, staring at the princess. "But I planned it all along! And I did it with the help of your former friend over here, the dark Prince Ungast! I used my powers to guide Ungast to the Viper! I had you take me to the Serpent Sea!"

The Ninns stepped forward slowly.

"Our leader has . . . returned?" said one.

Sparr glared at the red-faced soldiers. "Your leader *has* returned. Bigger, badder, and, if I may say so, better-looking than before! Watch out, universe. Sparr is back!"

He raised his fists to the air, and blasts of hot, red sparks shot up over the summit like fireworks. Sparr laughed and laughed.

A call that could be heard for miles exploded among the red-faced warriors. The Ninns raised their enormous, six-fingered hands to the dark sky and shouted at the top of their lungs, "All hail Lord Sparr!"

"I'll say!" said Sparr. "All hail me!"

Keeah barely had the strength to stand.

With Lord Sparr back — *evil* Lord Sparr! — and on Gethwing's side, Droon truly was doomed.

"Oh, don't be so sad, kiddies," the sorcerer said to the children. "Just think how much fun Gethwing, Ungast, Neffu, and I will have. Our Crown of Wizards will rule Droon. In five days, we shall be at the gates of Jaffa City. And then you'll see what we're really like."

And there, at the summit of Barrowbork, Lord Sparr took his place in the dark circle of Princess Neffu, Prince Ungast, and Emperor Gethwing.

"My Crown of Wizards," said the dragon. "Behold us, and bow to our majesty!"

A beam of light shot from the Viper to one, then the other, the third, and the fourth, creating a sizzling crown of light.

"The dark forces of old Goll are alive again!" cried Gethwing.

Keeah, Neal, and Julie stood opposite the four fearsome wizards, trembling in fear.

But they did not bow.

"The next time you see us, you won't believe our powers," said Ungast.

"Powers beyond your wildest nightmares," said Sparr.

"The conquest of Droon is at hand," said Gethwing. "And after Droon, I have my sights on another goal!"

Sparr's thin lips curled into a cruel smile. "Soon the Upper World will be ours, too!"

Neffu stepped forward. "And this will help," she said. She tore the pouch of magic dust from Keeah's belt. "This makes the staircase appear. Kee-kee, you don't mind if we use it just this once, do you?"

Gethwing laughed. "Send the Kindu!"

"Send them?" said Julie. "Where?"

"Where do you think?" said Ungast.

"But Eric's mother! The Upper World!" cried Neal.

Laughing, Neffu cast the powder far and wide until — *whoosh!* — the staircase appeared over the summit of Barrowbork.

The three dark hunters who had accompanied the prince to the treasure fortress bowed once and tramped up the stairs, carrying their stolen treasures in a sack.

"Bon voyage!" said Sparr.

"No, no, no!" shouted Julie. "You can't!"

"We just did," said Neffu with a scowl.

Keeah watched Prince Ungast. She could see the photograph inside his cloak.

But something was wrong.

She had put it in his left pocket. She knew she had. But now it was on the other side.

Had Ungast seen the photograph?

Her eyes grew wide. **Eric . . . ?**

There was no response.

"We are about to leave my fortress," said Gethwing. "My secret hideout. My —"

Bumblebee, said Keeah silently, watching Ungast's face intently. Then . . . there it was. The barest hint of a smile. It disappeared almost instantly.

"— Barrowbork," said the dragon.

Keeah saw Ungast survey the Dark Lands below. He rubbed his eyes. His forehead wrinkled. He squinted. Then his fingers reached to his temples as if to grasp something.

He dropped his hand, but it was enough for Keeah.

Eyeglasses! she said to herself. *He reached for his glasses!*

Eric? she spoke silently. **Are you there?**

She waited, waited, hoping against hope. There was no response.

Until . . . soft words sounded in her mind.

Hush, Keeah. I'm here.

It was the voice of Eric Hinkle.

Eric! she said. *Is it really you?*

Five days, he said. *I can hold them off for five days. Bring me the Moon Medallion. It's the only way to save Droon. If you can't . . . then it's over.*

Gethwing flapped his four giant wings and rose above the summit. "In five days, we meet at Jaffa City!" he boomed. "To claim our true throne!"

And the four dark figures — Neffu, Ungast, Sparr, and Gethwing — soared up together. They disappeared in the smoky distance.

At the dragon's command, the armies joined one another, the largest mass of beasts, wraiths, Ninns, and wingwolves ever known. And they moved across the land toward Jaffa City.

In a matter of moments, Julie, Neal, Keeah, and Galen were left alone at Barrowbork's summit.

Keeah blinked away her tears. "Eric is not gone! He is there. I heard him. He's fooling Gethwing! We have five days to help him stop Gethwing. All is not lost. It's not. There is hope!"

"Yet I must leave you," Galen whispered. "Anusa the genie will come for me, and I must journey from you. Soon. Very soon."

"Let's find Max and race to Zorfendorf," said Keeah, gently holding Galen's hand. "There we'll decide what to do next. We have to hurry now."

"And we need to find the hunters!" said Neal.

With that, Neal and Julie charged up the stairs, as Keeah helped the old wizard away from Barrowbork to join the distant king.

"Hurry!" said Julie, leaping up the steps as fast as she could go. At the top step, she and Neal jumped up for the basement light.

Click!

They charged into the basement, then stopped.

They saw footprints.

Thin, sharp, ghostlike shapes, the prints were barely noticeable except for a faint silvery glow on the cement. They led upstairs and into the house.

Neal gulped. "The hunters are here!"